Duck
for Turkey Day

Jacqueline Jules   Illustrated by Kathryn Mitter

Albert Whitman & Company, Morton Grove, Illinois

To Carla Heymsfeld, a wonderful friend and writer.—J.J.

Library of Congress Cataloging-in-Publication Data

Jules, Jacqueline, 1956-
Duck for Turkey Day / Jacqueline Jules ; illustrated by Kathryn Mitter.
p. cm.
Summary: When Tuyet finds out that her Vietnamese family is having duck rather than
turkey for Thanksgiving dinner, she is upset until she finds out that other children in her class
did not eat turkey either.
ISBN 978-0-8075-1734-5
[1. Thanksgiving Day—Fiction. 2. Vietnamese Americans—Fiction. 3. Schools—Fiction.]
I. Mitter, Kathy, ill. II. Title.
PZ7.J92947Du 2009 [E]—dc22 2008055537

The design is by Carol Gildar.

For more information about Albert Whitman & Company,
please visit our web site at www.albertwhitman.com.

To get ready for Thanksgiving, Tuyet's class sang turkey songs. They made pine cone turkeys. They talked about Pilgrims and Native Americans.

"See you on Monday," Mrs. Cook said when the bell rang. "Have a great Turkey Day!"

Tuyet was excited about the Thanksgiving holiday. They would get three days off from school! But there was something important she had to talk to Mama about.

"Mama," Tuyet said as soon as she got home. "We need a turkey for Thanksgiving."

"No, we don't." Mama smiled. "We'll buy duck at the market."

"But everybody else will have turkey!" Tuyet said.

That afternoon, Ba Noi arrived from New York. Tuyet hugged her grandmother. "We're having duck for Thanksgiving dinner."

"I know," Ba Noi said. "We're using my recipe from Vietnam."

"Everybody else has turkey."

"Our family likes duck better," Ba Noi answered.

Back home, Tuyet went to her bedroom. She pulled her pine cone turkey out of her book bag.

"Mama and Ba Noi don't know the rules about Thanksgiving," she told the turkey.

Tuyet counted the money in her wallet. Twelve dollars.
It might be enough to buy a turkey at the market.

On Wednesday, Mama drove Tuyet and Ba Noi to the
Saigon Supermarket. Tuyet held her wallet in her hand.
Inside the store, she saw all sorts of vegetables.
She saw fish, pork, duck, chicken, beef, shrimp—but
no turkey anywhere.

Tuyet watched Ba Noi talk to the man at the counter.
He handed her a package.

"This duck will be delicious," Ba Noi told Tuyet.

Tuyet put her wallet in her pocket.

The next morning, good cooking smells filled the house. Tuyet peeked into the kitchen. Soon all kinds of food would be put out on the table. But there would be no turkey!

Tuyet ran to her room and brought back the pine cone turkey she had made in school. *Now there's a turkey on the table*, she said to herself.

She felt a little better.

Her cousins, Kimily and Minh, came over at three.
They played tag outside until the grownups were ready
to eat.

"Did you know we're having duck for Thanksgiving
dinner?" Tuyet asked her cousins.

"Yum!" said Kimily. "I love duck!"

"With spicy sauce!" said Minh.

Mama called them inside for dinner. Kimily and Minh ran up the steps. But Tuyet walked slowly. Was she the only one who knew that Thanksgiving was Turkey Day?

"I'd like to give thanks," Daddy said when they sat down at the table. "For our home and our family."

"For America," Ba Noi said, raising her glass.

"For all this good food," Minh said, picking up his fork. "I'm hungry!"

Everyone laughed and passed their plates to be filled. Tuyet had a little bit of everything. But she had seconds of the duck. She loved the spicy sauce and dark meat.

When it was time to say goodbye, everybody hugged.
"What a great Thanksgiving Day!" Kimily told Tuyet.
It had been wonderful, Tuyet thought, with lots of good
food and family fun. But what would Mrs. Cook say about
eating duck on Turkey Day?

On Monday morning, Mrs. Cook gathered the class on the story rug.

"How was your Turkey Day?" she asked.

Tyler raised his hand. "My grandpa came. We played football!"

"That's nice," Mrs. Cook said. "Who else saw grandparents?"

Tuyet raised her hand along with other classmates.

"Who saw cousins?"
Mrs. Cook asked.
    Tuyet raised her hand again.
    "Who'd like to talk about
their dinner?"

Mrs. Cook looked around the room. Tuyet put her hand down. Tears burned her eyes.

"Is something wrong?" Mrs. Cook asked gently.

"We didn't have turkey!" Tuyet blurted out. "We had duck!"

For a few moments, the class was quiet. Then Phong raised his hand.

"We didn't have turkey, either," he said. "We had noodles and chicken."

"We had lamb," Tarek said.

"We had roast beef," Jonathan said.

"We had enchiladas," Carolina said.

"We had tofu turkey!" Amy said.

Mrs. Cook smiled. "It doesn't matter what you eat on Thanksgiving, as long as you have a good time with family and friends."